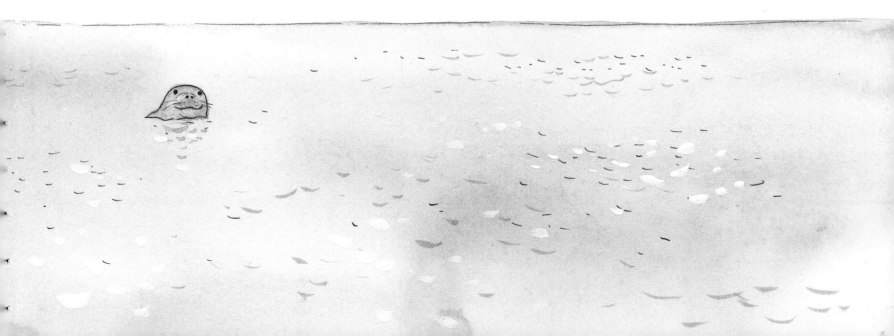

For Joe, Ed, and Benjamin —L.C.
For Sophie, Eddie, Johnny, John, and Sergio —B.F.

AUTHOR'S NOTE

Many years ago, I traveled to New Zealand to swim across three lakes near Mount Cook. Before heading home to California, I took a walk along the Avon River, which flows through the city of Christchurch. A boy and a girl were standing on its banks, and they asked me if I was looking for Elizabeth.

"Who?" I replied.

The boy, Michael, explained that Elizabeth was a very lovely elephant seal who had decided to live in Christchurch. Then Michael and his sister, Maggie, went on to tell me the wonderful story of Elizabeth, Queen of the Seas. And when they were done, I knew that one day I would have to pass Elizabeth's story on to you.

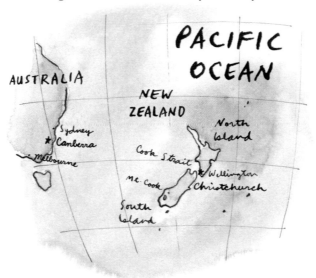

The author and illustrator wish to thank elephant seal expert Cory Champagne of the University of California, Santa Cruz, for his help with this story.

Text copyright © 2014 by Lynne Cox
Jacket and interior illustrations copyright © 2014 by Brian Floca
All rights reserved. Published in the United States by Schwartz & Wade Books, an imprint of Random House Children's Books, a division of Random House LLC, New York, a Penguin Random House Company. Schwartz & Wade Books and the colophon are trademarks of Random House LLC.
Visit us on the Web! randomhouse.com/kids
Educators and librarians, for a variety of teaching tools, visit us at RHTeachersLibrarians.com

Library of Congress Cataloging-in-Publication Data
Cox, Lynne.
Elizabeth, queen of the seas / Lynne Cox ; illustrated by Brian Floca.—1st ed.   p. cm.
ISBN 978-0-375-85888-8 (trade)
ISBN 978-0-375-95888-5 (glb)
ISBN 978-0-375-98769-4 (ebook)

1. Elephant seals—New Zealand—Christchurch—Juvenile literature. 2. Human-animal relationships—New Zealand—Christchurch—Juvenile literature. 3. Christchurch (N.Z.)—Social life and customs—Juvenile literature. I. Floca, Brian, ill. II. Title.
QL737.P64C69 2012
599.79 40929—dc23
2011023586

The text of this book is set in Bodoni Old Face.

The illustrations were rendered in pen-and-ink and watercolor.

MANUFACTURED IN CHINA
10 9 8 7 6 5 4 3 2 1
First Edition

Elizabeth,
Queen of the Seas

By Lynne Cox

Illustrated by Brian Floca

schwartz & wade books · new york

There was once a lovely elephant seal who lived in the city. Most elephant seals live in the ocean, in salt water. They sleep on rocky coasts and lie along sandy beaches. But this seal was different. She swam in the sweet, shallow waters of the Avon River where it flowed through the heart of the city of Christchurch, New Zealand.

When the seal grew tired, she'd pull herself onto the shore with her front flippers, then haul her back flippers up behind her.

Moving up the soft shore like a giant inchworm, she'd stretch herself out on the long, cool grass and take a nap in the bright sunshine.

And when she got hot, she'd use her flippers to
toss huge clumps of cold, wet mud onto her back.

The seal's coat was silvery brown. She was eight feet long—as long as a long surfboard—and she weighed twelve hundred pounds—as much as fifteen Labrador retrievers. The people of Christchurch knew there was something very special about her. She was strong and powerful and regal—like Elizabeth, the Queen of England.

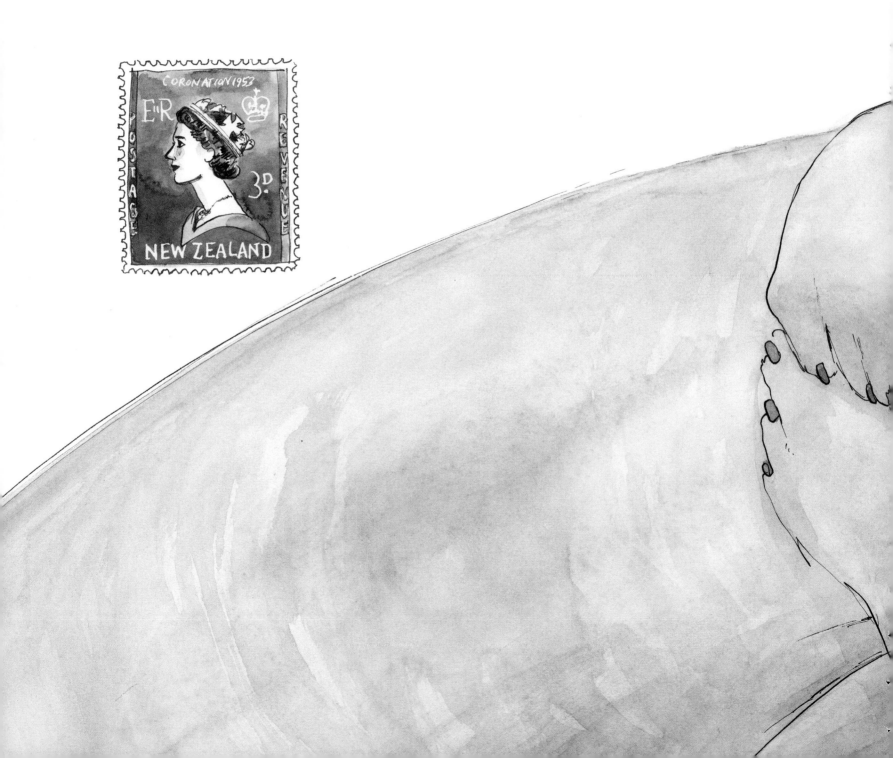

And so they named her

Elizabeth, Queen of the Seas.

There was one small boy named Michael who looked for the elephant seal every day on his way to school, and again on his way home. Even on weekends he walked beside the slow, swaying waters, hoping to spot Elizabeth's head bobbing above the current or see her body resting on the riverbank. Though Michael knew never to get too close to her—after all, she was a wild animal—he liked to call out her name.

And if Elizabeth was near, she'd turn and look at Michael with her dark brown eyes,

snort once to clear the water from her nostrils, and once again, as if to say hello.

Early one morning, when the grass was still wet,
Elizabeth hauled herself up, up, up to the top of the
riverbank . . . and stretched out across the two-lane road.

Maybe she liked the feel of the warm firmness under her
belly, or maybe it was the sunshine fanning out across her back.
But whatever it was, she decided to stay.

Suddenly, there was a screeching of brakes. Elizabeth moved forward as quickly as a twelve-hundred-pound animal with flippers for legs can.

BANG!

The car hit a rock and dented its fender. Elizabeth threw herself across the road.

Another screech. A second car just missed
running over her back flippers.

Elizabeth, Queen of the Seas,
slid down the riverbank and
belly-flopped into the water.

"ELIZABETH ESCAPES DEATH BY A FLIPPER'S BREADTH!"
the Christchurch newspaper proclaimed the next day.

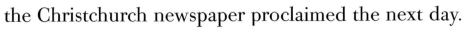

All over town, people were talking.
Some were afraid Elizabeth would climb
into the road again and be hit by a car.

Others worried that she'd cause a terrible accident when cars swerved to avoid her.

They decided that maybe it would be better for Elizabeth to live with other elephant seals. If she lived far away from the city, she wouldn't be a danger to anyone.

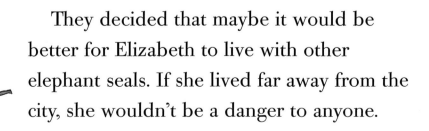

So one day, a group of volunteers in a small
motorboat waited until Elizabeth was in the river,
then approached her, slowly, and gently looped a
rope around her large body.

As they towed Elizabeth down the Avon River, a boy watched from the bridge. "Don't take my elephant seal away!" Michael cried. "This is where she belongs!"

But the boat went on, towing Elizabeth out past the silty, brownish-green river mouth into the cold, dark ocean.

At last the boat reached a sandy beach where other elephant seals lived. There the crew set her free.

Before Elizabeth, hundreds of elephant seals lay squished together. Huge males, three times the size of the females, were roaring, bellowing, and belching. Mother seals called to their babies with squeaks and squawks and whimpers, and babies squeaked back.

Maybe it was because the beach was too crowded and noisy, maybe she missed Christchurch, or maybe there was some other reason that we can never know, but Elizabeth chose not to stay.

Instead, the Queen of the Seas turned around and made herself as streamlined as possible, tucking her front flippers close in to her sides so that she could move swiftly through the water. Back across the cold open ocean she swam . . .

and into the sweet, warm Avon River. Still on she swam, past the wispy willow trees that lined the shore, until she reached her favorite sunbathing spot by the bridge. There she hauled herself out onto the riverbank and lay across the warm road.

Elizabeth! You're home!

Michael shouted.

And Elizabeth lifted her big head, looked at
him with her dark brown eyes, snorted loudly
once, then snorted again.

It wasn't long before people all over Christchurch were running down to the riverbank or jumping on their bicycles to see Elizabeth.

The traffic safety officers called the boat
crew, who caught Elizabeth yet again.

This time they towed Elizabeth to a
seal colony far, far away from the city.

Each day Michael looked for his friend on the way to school and on his way home. Each day there was no one there to greet him.

But then one day, miraculously, Elizabeth was back, looking up at Michael and snorting before pulling her great body out to sun herself along the road.

When Elizabeth was taken away the next time, people thought they would never see her again.

The boat towed Elizabeth hundreds of miles from Christchurch before letting her go. And as the seal pulled herself out of the ocean water onto some large rocks along the shore, the boat turned and headed back to Christchurch.

A month passed. Michael and his friends rode their bikes and swam in the river.

They explored, built forts, and lay in the wild fields outside Christchurch, reading great books. And always they watched for Elizabeth.

A second month passed.

And then almost a third.

Michael watched the water,
and he wished upon the stars.

And then one warm summer morning, Elizabeth was back.

There in the water beneath the bridge was the
beautiful elephant seal who weighed as much as
fifteen Labrador retrievers.

Welcome home, Elizabeth!

Michael shouted.

Elizabeth looked at him with her dark
brown eyes, snorted once, and once again.

Michael ran to tell his friends, who told their families, who all came down to the spot on the bridge. Looking out into the sun-speckled water, they cried,

Welcome home,

Queen of the Seas!

The people of Christchurch loved Elizabeth, and so they decided to put up a sign on the road where she liked to sleep. It was bright yellow with large black letters on it that said:

To this day, townspeople wonder
how Elizabeth managed to travel so far.

They know she must have swum through
huge waves and against strong currents.

She must have swum tired
but still kept on swimming.

She must even have swum while
she slept, night after day after night.

And they like to imagine that at last, when she
reached the mouth of the Avon River, she swam upon
a stream of moonlight until she reached the shore.

There was once a lovely elephant seal
who lived in the city.

And that is exactly where she belonged.

SOME FACTS ABOUT SOUTHERN ELEPHANT SEALS LIKE ELIZABETH

Elephant seals are named for their huge size and the trunk-like nose of the male, or bull. Bulls can be as long as fifteen feet and weigh up to four tons—that's 8,000 pounds! (The females are much smaller, though still over 2,000 pounds.) All dive deep into the sea to catch fish. They have big eyes that collect light to help them see in the dark world below, and sensitive whiskers to detect movement. Elephant seals eat squid, cuttlefish, and octopus, including deep-sea varieties that glow in the dark, making them easier to spot. Elephant seals also eat small sharks. Most of the seals' lives are spent looking for food.

But for a few months each year, elephant seals are too busy to find food, and they fast—they don't eat or drink anything at all. This happens during the breeding season, while the males defend their territory and the females nurse the pups, and then again later in the year, while the animals molt—shed and grow new fur.

Since they are mammals, elephant seals need to come to the water's surface to breathe. Still, they can stay underwater for up to two hours, accomplishing this by lowering their heart rate to as little as four beats per minute. When an elephant seal needs air, it swims to the surface, lifts its head out of the water, and takes in a big breath, making a huge snorting sound. The seal catches its breath for two or three minutes, then dives again.

Recently, elephant seals have become our aquanauts. Scientists attach computerized tags to their heads to collect information about conditions in parts of the oceans where we can't easily go. With the help of the elephant seals, we can explore the mysteries of the deep as never before.

If you'd like to learn more about elephant seals, two good websites to visit are topp.org and nationalgeographic.com/animals/mammals/elephant-seal.html.

Fairfax Media / The Press

The real Elizabeth, Queen of the Seas